R.L. STINE

Goosebumps

TERROR TRIPS

graphix

AN IMPRINT OF

■SCHOLASTIC

NEW YORK   TORONTO   LONDON   AUCKLAND   SYDNEY   MEXICO CITY   NEW DELHI   HONG KONG   BUENOS AIRES

The Goosebumps book series created by Parachute Press, Inc.
Copyright © 2007 Scholastic Inc.
Cover, center & illustrations, pages 5–46, 137 © 2007 Jill Thompson
Cover, right & illustrations, pages 47–87, 138 © 2007 Jamie Tolagson
Cover, left & illustrations, pages 89–136, 139 © 2007 Amy Kim Ganter

Based on "One Day at Horrorland," © 1994 Scholastic Inc.; "A Shocker on Shock Street," © 1995 Scholastic Inc.; and "Deep Trouble," © 1994 Scholastic Inc.

Library of Congress Cataloging-in-Publication Data available
ISBN-13: 978-0-439-85777-2 / ISBN-10: 0-439-85777-5 (hardcover)
ISBN 0-439-85780-5 (paperback)

16 15 14 13   15 16 17 18/0
First edition, March 2007
Edited by Sheila Keenan
Book design by Richard Amari
Creative Director: David Saylor
Printed in China 38

ONE DAY AT HORRORLAND

ADAPTED AND ILLUSTRATED BY

Jill Thompson

9

YUCK! WHAT IS IT? MY FACE-?

IT'S SO GROSS! MY FACE - IT **HURTS!**

IT'S LIKE **HOT, STICKY COBWEBS!!**

AND THEN A FLARE OF BRIGHT LIGHT MADE ME SHUT MY EYES.

I FORCED MY EYES OPEN....

! o

GREAT SPECIAL EFFECTS!

WHEN DOES THIS RIDE **END?**

SWOOSH!

HEY, GUYS!

WHERE'VE YOU **BEEN?**

WHERE'VE **WE** BEEN? WHERE'VE **YOU** BEEN?

RIGHT **HERE.** I DIDN'T KNOW WHERE I WAS.

I **THINK** THIS IS THE OTHER SIDE OF THE PARK OR SOMETHING SO I JUST WAITED FOR YOU.

BUT WE **SEARCHED** **EVERYWHERE**!

SO?

SO, IF THEY'RE **NOT** IN THE PARK, SOMETHING **BAD** HAPPENED TO THEM.

WHAT DO YOU MEAN, LIZZY?

I MEAN, **MAYBE** THIS **PLACE** REALLY IS **EVIL**!

THAT'S CRAZY!

AND MAYBE THE **HORRORS** OR SOME- BODY **DID** SOMETHING TO MOM AND DAD.

I HAVE SUCH A BAD **FEELING** ABOUT THIS PLACE.

A **REAL BAD** FEELING!

LYING ON MY BACK I COULDN'T SEE THE OTHERS OVER THE COFFIN SIDES.

THIS IS **NICE**. VERY RELAXING.

IT'S **BORING**!

WHERE'S THE **SCARY** PART?

DO YOU THINK THE COFFIN IS ON SOME KIND OF TRACK?

IS THAT A **HAWK** UP IN THE SKY? CAN EVERYONE **SEE** IT?

IT'S **NOT A** HAWK. I'LL BET IT'S A **VULTURE**!

IT SEES THE COFFINS...

...AND IT'S WAITING TO **EAT OUR FLESH**!

LUKE! **WHERE** DO YOU GET THESE **HIDEOUS** IDEAS?

MAYBE LUKE SHOULD **LIVE** IN HORRORLAND! WE COULD GET HIM ONE OF THOSE **MONSTER** COSTUMES. AND HE'D **FIT** RIGHT IN!

SLAP

ALL OF IT. I'M SAD TO SAY IT'S TIME TO SAY—GOOD-BYE TO OUR SPECIAL GUESTS THIS WEEK.

...SAD.

SAYING GOOD-BYE IS ALWAYS—

SO WE TRY TO HAVE A LITTLE FUN WITH OUR FAREWELLS.

WE COULDN'T RUN, THEY HAD US SURROUNDED.

THEN—I HAD A CRAZY IDEA.

PINCH THEM!

FWOOOSH

THE "NO PINCHING" SIGNS WE THOUGHT WERE SO STUPID—

ALL VERY SERIOUS...

RIDES... SIGNS ALL OF...

I HAD TO TRY IT.

I'M THE MAD PINCHER!

THEY WERE SERIOUS!

44

A SHOCKER ON SHOCK STREET

ADAPTED AND ILLUSTRATED BY

Jamie Tolagson

The End

a Shocker Studios Production

...IT WILL BE USED AT THE *SHOCKER STUDIO* TOUR.

YOU'VE BEEN WORKING ON THE TOUR FOR FOUR YEARS. IS IT FINALLY GOING TO OPEN?

YES. BUT BEFORE IT DOES, I WANT YOU TWO TO TEST IT OUT.

YOU MEAN IT?

YES! YES! YES!

DAD, THE *SHOCK STREET* MOVIES ARE THE *BEST!* AWESOME! IS IT SCARY?

THE *REAL* SHOCK STREET? YOU GET TO RIDE DOWN THE REAL STREET WHERE THEY MAKE THE MOVIES?

YES. THE REAL SHOCK STREET, AND I WANT YOU TO GO BY YOURSELVES. I THINK THAT WILL MAKE IT MORE EXCITING FOR YOU.

WHOA! TAKE IT EASY. YOU'LL BLOW A FUSE!

ARF! ARF!

MAYBE WE SHOULD PUT HIM ON A LEASH.

YOU HAVE TO TAKE THE AUTOMATED TRAMCAR.

YOU MEAN WE CAN'T WALK ON SHOCK STREET?

I'LL BE WAITING FOR YOU WHEN YOU GET BACK.

I WANT A FULL REPORT ON WHAT YOU LIKE AND DON'T LIKE.

DON'T WORRY IF THINGS DON'T WORK EXACTLY RIGHT. THERE ARE STILL A FEW BUGS.

COOL!!! CAN WE RIDE IN FRONT?

SIT ANYWHERE YOU WANT. THIS WHOLE RIDE IS JUST FOR YOU.

ALL RIIIGHT!!!

LET'S GET THIS SHOW ON THE ROAD. REMEMBER: STAY IN THE TRAMCAR, NO MATTER WHAT!

FIRST STOP, THE HAUNTED HOUSE OF HORROR!

THIS IS AWESOME! WE'RE GOING TO SEE ALL THE GREAT CREATURES FROM THE SHOCKER MOVIE.

I WANT TO SEE WOLF BOY, WOLF GIRL...

...THE PIRANHA PEOPLE, CAPTAIN SICK, THE GREAT GOPHER MUTANT...

58

CLACK

CLACK

CLACK-I-TY

CLACK

WHOA! THAT WAS EXCELLENT!

I'M GOING TO TELL YOUR DAD THAT ROLLERCOASTER RIDE WAS THE BEST!

Y-YEAH. I-IT WAS KIND OF FUN...AND SCARY.

HEY. WHERE ARE WE?

THERE'S NOTHING AROUND HERE. WHY DID WE STOP?

JOSH...

THERE'S SOMEONE THERE!

WHEN I SAW THEM CREEPING OUT, I THOUGHT I'D HAVE A COW!

IT'S JUST A BUNCH OF ACTORS IN COSTUMES.

BUT THEY LOOKED SO REAL. THE TOADINATOR'S HANDS WERE REALLY *SLIMY*, APE FACE'S *FUR* WAS SO REAL.

THE MASKS WERE AWESOME. HOW DO THEY GET INTO THOSE COSTUMES? I DIDN'T SEE ANY BUTTONS OR ZIPPERS!

THEYR'E MOVIE COSTUMES, SO THEY'RE BETTER THAN REGULAR COSTUMES.

PLEASE REMAIN IN THE CAR AT ALL TIMES.

YOUR NEXT STOP WILL BE THE *CAVE OF THE LIVING CREEPS!!!!*

THINK THERE ARE BATS IN THERE?

BATS ARE UGLY AND DISGUSTING. I HATE THEM.

LOOK OVER THERE! A *VAMPIRE BAT!*

HUH? WHERE?

YOU'RE NOT FUNNY.

HA! HA! HA! HA! HA! HA! HA!

THAT WAS TOTALLY *GROSS!* DO YOU THINK THOSE DISGUSTING WHITE WORMS WERE ALIVE?

OF COURSE NOT. THEY WERE ROBOTS OR SOMETHING.

I'M NOT SURE. THE WAY THEY WRIGGLED AROUND—

EVERYTHING HERE IS FAKE. JUST ASK YOUR FATHER.

I'M NOT SO SURE...

WHY DID WE STOP HERE? IT'S JUST A BIG EMPTY CAVE.

HEY! CAN ANYBODY HEAR US?

DRIP

DRIP

DRIP

DRIP

I THINK THIS TRAM IS STUCK OR SOMETHING.

YOU MEAN WE'RE *STRANDED* HERE?

PLUNK

PLUNK

PLUNK

WE CAN FIND A WAY OUT.

BUT WE'RE NOT SUPPOSED TO LEAVE THE TRAM. GET BACK IN. IF IT SHOULD START UP...

I THINK IT BROKE DOWN.

YOU'D BETTER CLIMB DOWN, WE HAVE TO WALK.

WALK? IN THIS CREEPY, DARK CAVE? NO WAY, JOSH!

DRIP

PLUNK

DRIP

PLUNK

BEHIND YOU!

WHOAA!!

CHITTER

CLICK

WHAT IS THAT THING?

IT'S A— PRAYING MANTIS!

HA-HA! OF COURSE! WHY SHOULD WE BE SCARED? IT'S A BIG ROBOT.

HUH? BUT, JOSH.

IT ISN'T REAL. IT'S PROGRAMMED TO WALK UP TO THE TRAM. IT'S ALL ON A COMPUTER.

IT'S...UH... REALLY LIFELIKE.

CHITTER

YOUR DAD IS A GENIUS AT THIS STUFF!

HE SAID THERE WERE STILL SOME BUGS. HA-HA-HA! GREAT-LOOKING ROBOTS!

SCREEE

DRIP

CLACK

DRIP

DRIP

67

I WISH I HAD A CAMERA.

I'D REALLY LIKE A PICTURE OF ME STANDING IN THE MANGLER'S LOT.

...OR EVEN *BETTER!*

HEY! WAIT UP!

...A PHOTO OF ME STANDING IN THE ACTUAL SET WHERE THEY FILMED *CEMETERY ON SHOCK STREET.*

LET'S GO, IT'S GETTING LATE.

YOU DIDN'T USED TO BE SUCH A TOTAL WIMP!

I-I JUST HAVE A *BAD* FEELING ABOUT THIS CEMETERY.

IT'S PART OF THE TOUR.

BUT THE GATE IS CLOSED!

HA HA HA HA HA

JOSH-?

HA HA HA HA HA

JOSH? WHERE ARE YOU?

IT'S A GHOST TRAM...A *GHOST TRAM* FILLED WITH SKELETONS!

BUT WE RODE IN IT!

I'M SICK OF MYSTERIES! I'M SICK OF BEING SCARED!

YOUR FATHER CAN EXPLAIN IT ALL!

I DON'T WANT HIM TO EXPLAIN IT. I JUST WANT TO GET AWAY FROM HERE!

JOSH, LOOK! WE MUST BE HEADING BACK TO THE MAIN PLATFORM! YES!

OH NO.

WE'RE BACK ON *SHOCK STREET!*

OOOOOOO!

I DON'T WANT TO BE HERE!

RUN!

THE TOUR—IT'S TOTALLY MESSED UP! THE CREATURES... THEY'RE *ALIVE!* THEY TRIED TO HURT US!

IT WASN'T LIKE A RIDE! IT WAS REALLY *GROSS!*

WHOA! WHOA!!

IT WAS ALL SPECIAL EFFECTS. DIDN'T THEY EXPLAIN WE WERE FILMING YOUR REACTIONS?

MY DAD DESIGNED THIS STUDIO TOUR. HE DIDN'T TELL US ABOUT ANY MOVIE BEING FILMED.

IT'S OKAY. WE JUST GOT A LITTLE SCARED.

MY DAD MUST BE REALLY WORRIED. CAN YOU TELL US HOW TO GET TO THE MAIN PLATFORM?

NO PROBLEM. GO RIGHT IN THAT DOOR STRAIGHT THROUGH *SHOCKRO'S HOUSE OF SHOCKS.*

WON'T WE GET SHOCKED WITH *20 MILLION VOLTS* OF ELECTRICITY IN THERE, LIKE THE MOVIE?

THE HOUSE IS JUST A SET. IT'S PERFECTLY SAFE. GO OUT THE BACK AND YOU'LL SEE THE MAIN BUILDING.

DEEP TROUBLE

ADAPTED AND ILLUSTRATED BY

Amy Kim Ganter

There I was, William Deep, Jr. of Baltimore, Maryland, swimming two hundred feet under the sea on the hunt of my life.

The hunt for...

the Great White Stingray!

My oxygen tank!

Someone must have tampered with it! I had to surface -- FAST!

Help me! NO AIR!! Someone -- cut off-- tank--

Get real, Billy!

I'd better go see what this is about.

I wonder if Dr. D. would let me do some more snorkeling this afternoon. Was I scared? Yes.

But I was also determined to prove I wasn't crazy.

I don't care how you do it, Dr. Deep...

...but I want you to find that mermaid!

Shh!
Don't make
any noise!!

What do you
think you're
doing?

...

kruu~!
~kru~!

You can't keep her in there!
Look how unhappy she is!

CLICK

Your uncle's worked his whole life
for a discovery like this.
It would break his heart if
you let her go.

What about
her heart?

A few hours later...

Want some lunch? I made marinated squid.

I'll bring some bread and iced tea!

Kru!

?

You are hungry, aren't you?

CHOMP!!

That night...

zZZz -- Mmph?

chg~chg~ chg~

WHUMPH!!

THUD

?

The mermaid!

THMP
THMP
THMP
THMP

Stay away --or you'll get hurt.

Dr. D!!

SLAM

123

Maybe they need some help.

The mermaids are setting her free.

Come on, mermaids! Hurry!

What do you think you're doing?

Why aren't you dead?

Give us back the mermaid!

Finders keepers.

You've made a long trip for nothing. And now look--

--your boat is on fire.

Get the mermaid aboard. Let's get out of here.

FWOOM!!

FWWSS

FWWSHH

Billy -- get a life jacket! Sheena -- find the bucket. Throw water on the flames -- hurry!

POOMF

Alexander! Help us!

...

We'll look for her tomorrow. We know where to find her now.

Oh no! After all this, is Dr. D. going to catch the mermaid again and give her to the zoo?

The next morning...

Do you think the mermaid went back to the lagoon?

S CASSANDRA

Probably. That's where she lives.

Sheena...

?

If someone gave you a million dollars, would you show them where the mermaid lives?

No. Not if they wanted to capture her.

Me neither.

That's what I don't get.

Dr. D's a great guy. I just can't believe he'd-

VVVRRMMmm

CHG CHG CHG CHG CHG

...!

The zoo people!

We had word from the fishermen on Santa Anita that you found the mermaid. We're ready to take her now.

Here is a check for one million dollars. We made it out to you and the Cassandra Research Lab!

You sent me on a wild goose chase. I searched every inch of the lagoon and the surrounding waters.

My equipment can pick up the tiniest minnows.

Mermaids do not exist.

But what about the fishermen's stories?

Are you sure about this?

Completely sure. Mermaids are fantasy creatures.

We respect your opinion, Dr. Deep. You're the leading expert on exotic sea creatures...

...that's why we came to you in the first place.

Then I hope you'll take my advice and drop your hunt for a mermaid.

I guess we'll have to.

Thanks for trying, Dr. Deep.

VVRRRMMMM

Dr. D!!

OOF!

You're the greatest!

From now on, none of us will say anything to anyone about mermaids, deal?

Deal!

I swore I'd never mention the mermaid to anyone.

But I wanted to see her one last time.

I wanted to say good-bye.

SPLISH

SLSH

Mermaid? Where are you?

It must be the mermaid!

MEET THE ARTIST
Jill Thompson

Jill Thompson has illustrated books for nearly every comic book publisher in the United States. She is the creator of the award-winning Scary Godmother series and lives in Chicago, Illinois.

Outline

To adapt *One Day at Horrorland*, Jill Thompson first read the book! Then, she re-read it and underlined all the major action that moved the story along. Sometimes she scribbled drawings in the margins of the book when she had an idea of what she wanted to draw.

Next, she made an outline, listing from 1-40 on a piece of graph paper, Page 1 was the beginning of the story. By page 40, the story had to be finished. After checking her list of the major action in the book, Jill edited out some parts of the story to make it fit the number of pages she had to work with.

Jill then drew small sketches called thumbnails to give herself an idea of how the action on each page would appear to the reader. Next she drew the story lightly in pencil on pages of two-ply Bristol board. At this stage, she also put the lettering on the pages by hand and drew the word balloons. Finally, she used india drawing ink and a Deleter brand manga pen set to finish the drawings and the lettering. After the ink dried, she erased any pencil lines that remained on the board. This is called cleaning up the page. Jill still does all of her drawing and lettering by hand on actual paperboard, but she's also learning how to do the lettering on her computer.

Jamie Tolagson

Jamie Tolagson lives in Victoria, British Columbia, Canada. He's been drawing comics for as long as he can remember. He still draws them the same way he did when he was a kid: with a pencil, pen, and paper. Jamie thinks it's more fun to draw on paper than on a computer, though sometimes he does use a computer to add gray tones to his work.

Jamie draws miniature versions of all his comics before he draws the full-sized versions. That way he can read the comic before anyone else to see if it's going the way he wants it to.

When he draws the full-sized comic, he first uses a # 2 pencil to sketch in what is happening on the pages; then he finishes the drawings with a fine-tipped ink pen. That's the part that takes up the most time. Normally, Jamie works a "size up," which means that he draws the pages twice as big as they will appear in the published comic. But for *A Shocker on Shock Street*, he decided to work at actual size, because it's closer to the size Jamie liked to draw at when he was a kid. Art school taught him to draw BIGGER, but he thinks it's fun to draw small, too — that way he can carry the drawing around and work on it anywhere: at the kitchen table, on the bus, wherever.

Jamie found working on this story to be a lot of fun. As he put it, "It's not often that I get to draw page after page of ghouls, ghosts, worms, skeletons, and giant salivating insects."

Penciled page

Amy Kim Ganter

Amy Kim Ganter is the creator of Sorcerers & Secretaries, a manga series published by Tokyopop, as well as the webcomic "Reman Mythology." She has also contributed to the acclaimed *Flight* anthology. Amy lives in Alhambra, California.

Amy read *Deep Trouble*, highlighted her favorite moments, and wrote the script for the comic adaptation at the same time.

Once the script was set, she drew layouts. These are rough sketches, drawn two pages per 8½ x 11 sheet of paper (**A**).

A

B

After the sketches were approved, it was time to ink and tone! She scanned in the layouts, increased the size on the computer so they fit one per 9 x 12 sheet of bristol paper, then printed out the layouts in light blue ink. She drew the linework directly on these bristol printouts using Micron pens. Her inks tend to look like something from a coloring book. See how much meaner the monster looks now? (**B**)

Now the artwork was ready for "special effects" known as gray-scaled tones, which Amy does with the computer program Photoshop. She also adds in the dialogue, which she had already typed in the computer and the sound effects, which she draws by hand. (**C**) Multiply this process 46 times and you have a cool Goosebumps Graphix story called *Deep Trouble*!

C

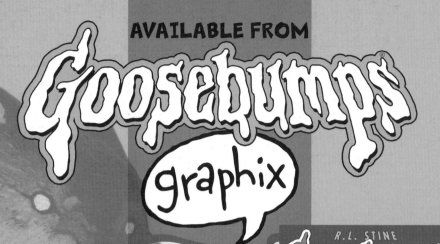

MORE GHOULISH TALES TO COME!

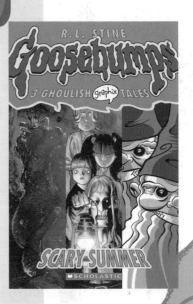

Wish that summer would never end? Not *THIS* summer!

Sandy beaches, tidal pools, shoreline caves . . . ghosts! A brother and sister's seaside vacation turns spooky at *Ghost Beach* by **Ted Naifeh**, creator of the creepy Courtney Crumrin series.

Someone's creeping through the garden, whispering nasty things, smashing melons, and squashing tomatoes, but those funky lawn ornaments can't move . . . right? **Dean Haspiel**, a veteran of Batman and Justice League comics and the acclaimed artist on *The Quitter*, knows just how to portray *The Revenge of the Lawn Gnomes*.

In his comic series like The Bakers and Plastic Man, **Kyle Baker** proves he's one funny artist. The perfect guy to draw a story about a summer camp where it's all fun and games and everybody's happy. Too happy . . . That's why one young girl is out to uncover *The Horror at Camp Jellyjam.*